# SPACE DUMPLINS

## CRAIG THOMPSON
### WITH COLOR BY DAVE STEWART

D1392155

LANCASHIRE COUNTY LIBRARY

30118132696505

ff

"They had dumplings, too; small, but substantial, symmetrically globular, and INDESTRUCTIBLE DUMPLINGS."

MOBY-DICK
BY HERMAN MELVILLE

First published in the UK in 2015
by Faber & Faber Ltd, Bloomsbury House,
74–77 Great Russell Street, London, WC1B 3DA
First published in the US in 2015
by Graphix, an imprint of Scholastic Inc.

Book design by Craig Thompson & Phil Falco; colour by Dave Stewart
Printed in China

All rights reserved
© Craig Thompson, 2015

The right of Craig Thompson to be identified as author of this work
has been asserted in accordance with Section 77 of the
Copyright Designs and Patents Act 1988

This book is a work of fiction. Names, characters, places, and incidents are either
the product of the author's imagination or are used fictitiously,
and any resemblance to actual persons, living or dead,
business establishments, events, or locales is entirely coincidental.

A CIP record for this book
is available from the British Library

ISBN 978–0–571–30307–6 (hardback)
ISBN 978–0–571–30308–3 (paperback)

2 4 6 8 10 9 7 5 3 1

STAR MAP

NAVIGATION · GYROMETER · SW

MAGNITUDES · ★ ✦ ✳ ✺ ❀

Mrs. Nurget, where's Livonia?

Playing at home and watching cartoons.

≡ SIGH ≡

Did you hear about the WHALE ATTACK?

No casualties. Just some storage sheds and an elementary school.

Too close for comfort.

The ROIDS might be next!

!

Cerulean Marlocke, you're exactly who I'm looking for.

Please, just "Cera."

I haven't yet finished this week's designs...

That's not my concern.

SHELL-TARR is transferring sectors to get out of harm's way, but I'm worried the FASHION FACTORY is gonna turn into a whale snack.

I can't afford to lose my most promising designer... so I got you THIS.

What is it, Mom?

WORK PERMIT

One scheduled station access per day. NINE-TO-FIVE. Mandatory exit, but it'll give you time at my official studio.

Th-that's my DREAM...

But...

Can I bring my daughter, Violet?

We can't use her.

NEW LABOR LAWS.

I already have one unpaid intern.

No, you see, she temporarily doesn't have a school...

I need her nearby to keep an eye on.

Sounds codependent.

CODEPENDENT?

Codependent.

NEXT TIME THERE MIGHT BE CASUALTIES!

SHUT IT, Tinder, and SURF THE LOG!

Sweetie, Tinder and I are HAULING A LOAD to the mill tonight.

WANT TO BE SURE IT'S ALL ACCOUNTED FOR.

PAYCHECK IN HAND, WE'LL START HUNTING FOR A NEW SCHOOL FOR VIOLET.

Hi, Daddy!

We're going to the SPACE STATION tomorrow!

THE WHAT?!

It's a promotion. ADAM ARNOLD wants me to bring designs directly to his studio on SHELL-TARR.

OH, FOR CRYING OUT LOUD...

I thought you'd be HAPPY for me.

JUST MIND YOURSELF AROUND THOSE PRETENTIOUS, PAMPERED PARASITES!

SPECIES?

Human.

What's a human family doing living OUTSIDE the Stations?

Your husband a SUBSPECIES?

My daddy's a LUMBERJACK!

Same difference. HEH HEH

All right. Child first for the RETINAL SCAN.

Welcome to SHELL·TARR™

the Ultimate in ASTRAL COMFORT & SECURITY®

If it's really so important, you can tour the school TOMORROW.

Today, let's focus on getting started at the studio.

What fashion NEEDS, Cerulean...

Please, just "CERA."

...is some of that EDGE your people have.

My PEOPLE?

Outer-space dwellers.

Real RUSTIC folk!

What are you doing?

' ' '

Do I... ...KNOW you?

My name's VIOLET. What's yours?

ELLIOT MARCEL OPGENORTH.

Now let me be.

What is THAT?

It's a book.

Don't you read?

Sure, I read.

My school has... HAD text vids ... uh ...the older models.

What kind of fabric is this?

It's PAPER. It's made from an extinct species of plant life.

DON'T CRINKLE IT!

This happens to be my PERSONAL DREAM JOURNAL!

DREAMS!

I had a dream that in the future all species live together in HARMONY!

Pedestrian.

What I'm documenting is far more complicated.

I'm DECODING the SYMBOLS within a spiritual PUZZLE.

MUSHROOMS!

MATHEMATICAL EQUATIONS!

ROTATING DISCS!

ORIGAMI UNICORNS!

Elliot is our BUTTON-RUNNER.

ha BUTT!

The lad has an eye for rare, hard-to-find BUTTONS, and knows where to obtain them.

MOSTLY ON THE INTERWEBS.

Elliot: husky, woven-leather BEETLE-BACK.

Perfect!

Cerulean, would you sew it?

But...

But what about my old friends?

You can make NEW friends.

Hi, my name's VIOLET.

HA HA Your clothes are HOMEMADE!

And your hair is dumb.

GASP!

I definitely want this to be MY recess!

Your WORK PERMIT has all the information needed for the registration.

Look, Mom-- It's ME!

The analysis takes a few hours. Check in with us after your workday.

Elliot the chicken, are you back here?

WRRR

WRRR

WRRR

WRRR

Don't meddle in my sanctuary.

Oh no...

Are you HANDICAPPED?

**C**HILD-
**H**ELPING
**A**ND
**P**ARENT-
**E**NABLING
**R**EPLACEMENT
**D**ISCIPLINARY
**R**OBOTIC
**O**PERATIONS
**N**ANNY
**E**NGINE

So what do you do for FUN on the station? Have you been to the PLAYGROUND?

Playgrounds are for BRUTES.

I prefer mental exercise.

HA HA MENTAL!

You must go crazy cooped up here all the time.

COOP? Please, no speciesist slurs.

Do you ever go on field trips?

Occasionally to Shell-tarr's LEEWARD side for their surplus of buttons.

No, I mean to other sectors and planets and GALAXIES!

Outer space doesn't interest me in the least bit. It's UNHYGIENIC and nightmarishly barren.

I only care for INNER SPACE.

So you're no FREE-RANGE CHICKEN, huh?

WHAT OPTIONS ARE LEFT?!

. . .

I don't wanna go to the station anymore. I want to join Daddy at his work.

What did we tell you, Violet?

Daddy's work is too dangerous.

MM

IT MIGHT GET MORE SO.

But I'm BORED.

And I'm lonely.

After dinner, let's make a PLAYDATE with friends from your old school.

HEY, V.M.!

Livonia! I miss you!

I GO TO INTERSTELLAR INNER CITY NOW!

We toured there!

WHY DIDN'T YOU ENROLL?

Oh, my parents thought it was... you know ...

WE HAVE A COOL NEW CLUB WHERE WE BEAT UP NERDS.

I just met a GENUINE NERD.

BRING HIM TO OUR CLUB MEETING, PLEASE!

HEY, WHY DOESN'T YOUR MOMMA WORK AT THE FACTORY WITH MY MOMMA ANYMORE?

She got promoted as a day laborer on SHELL-TARR.

WELL, LA-DEE-DA! GUESS YOU'RE TOO GOOD FOR US NOW.

That's not--

PEACE IN DUH GALACK'S EASE!

But...

What about STELLA?

She lives in our same trailer park.

No. Her family just moved for a job up in SECTOR 59.

Why look at me that way? They're called MOBILE HOMES. You go where work or life takes you.

That's not a HOME.

We have nowhere we belong.

Hey... I know an ol' buddy you haven't seen for a while...

...

Do you mean... AT THE SCRAPYARD?

Gar, that boy is a bad influence.

He's harmless.

Besides I need some SPARE PARTS.

SCHMASH

KSSHHHH

Zacchaeus?

...

Violet?

HEY, HEY.

Watch it with the COOTIES!

Has it been that long? You've grown SO TALL!

And you're ...

...the same size?

DON'T RUB IT IN.

SCHMASH

What are you doing?!

Compactor short-circuited again. Gordon has me on demolition duty.

C'mon ...

Help me BREAK THINGS.

You spent our hard-earned money...

...ON WHAT?!

It'll be good for Violet. She can learn MECHANICS.

A child needs to learn MATH and GRAMMAR!

Lots of good that does you when your spaceship breaks down and you're standing there with a calculator and your "dangling modifiers."

Well, mathematicians live on STATIONS so they don't have to worry about spaceships breaking down.

Plus, they're paid well enough to support a family.

Hey, now ...

A SPACE-BIKE, Garnett?!

You don't get it, do you?!

Not with you two FIGHTING all the time!

I just want things to go back to how they used to be.

Aww, Little Vee...

We're just frustrated that we haven't found you a new school yet.

≥SNIFF≤ We can return the trike and get our money back.

Nope.

...

## 02

MAG/
GYRO
NAV

MAGNITUDES:

# MISSING COMPONENT

When is Dad coming home?

Soon, sweetie.

He took a job that lasts a few more days than usual.

≶SIGH≶
I won't
sleep until
your father
is home.

Five minutes late...

Sorry, Adam, but I need to contact my husband.

Use my COM, if you must. I'll dock the long-distance charge from your wages.

Elliot?

Whatchya watchin'?

A·T·U·N·E

SPLI

ACROSS THE UNIVERSE NEWS AND ENTERTAINMENT!

Please, hush.

No connection.

Oh, well. Time to work.

CALL FAILED

I can't focus.

Gar might be in trouble.

Could you watch Violet for a moment?

The NURSLING?

MISSING PERSONS REGISTRY.

I need help finding my husband.

WHO'S ALSO MY DAD!

VIOLET! What are you doing here?

I thought I told you to wait at the studio!

≈Huff≈ BAD NEWS, Mom! ≈Huff≈ There's WHALE DIARRHEA out there!

This is no time for GROSS-OUTS, young lady!

HUSBAND'S EMPLOYER?

Oh, he works for INTER-STELLAR TIMBER that processes fuel nuggets for all the major energy corporations.

Then we'll contact the SAWMILL'S Human Species Resources Database.

MOM! This is serious! It's an ENVIRONMENTAL EMERGENCY!

Then it's even more important to get a hold of Daddy.

WHICH CONTRACTOR YOU LOOKIN' FOR?

Garnett Marlocke.

NO ONE BY THAT NAME HAS EVER WORKED FOR US.

What?! He's been with you SIXTEEN YEARS!

I demand to speak to the LUMBERJACK UNION!

I'm afraid there's nothing more we can help you with.

Mom, they aren't going to help. We should go on our own.

We'll try the MILITARY instead!

... ROBOTS with ANTHROPOMORPHIC CHARM!

They're loaded up with:

MISSILES, LASERS, PLASMA-GRENADES,

FLAME-THROWERS, HOWITZERS, BLUDGEONS,

BAZOOKAS, NUKES, AND SPIKY BALLS.

Then decorated with a friendly face,

and our CORPORATE LOGO.

Oh, but you're simply a day laborer. SHELL-TARR'S DEFENSE SYSTEM is only available to CITIZENS.

But...

See, Mom. I told you!

## WACK BLOTTER
### TOP OF THE LINE

## DEFENDOES
### COMPARISON BRAND

## SARTORI 2600
### MID-RANGE

## GALAXTICLES
### BUDGET OPTION

I can't afford any of these mercenaries. Even the ones you included for comedic relief.

Mrs. Marlocke?

I'm here on behalf of MISSING PERSONS REGISTRY.

Thank VENUS! Are you going to help me?

No. It's past CURFEW, and you neglected to punch the clock. We will now escort you off the premises.

Violet?

VIOLET!!

WHERE'S MY DAUGHTER?!

All noncitizens will be aboard the FERRY WHEEL.

Elliot, you're sweating up a downy FUNK.

CHILDREN SHOWING SIGNS OF DISTRESS, ENGAGE UPLIFTING ANTHEM.

♪ SMILE ♪ SMILE SMILE AWAY THE RAIN!

geeyah!

I think I'm having a PANIC ATTACK.

Well, I didn't rope you into this. It's your boss's fault.

He's not my boss.

Adam is like a SURROGATE FATHER.

Wait... Then where's your REAL father?

Three years now on LAB STAR.

He's a scientist.

Like my grandfather before him.

Chickens can be SCIENTISTS?

And what does YOUR father do?

He's a LUMBERJACK.

Lumberjack?

Yeah. He transports WHALE POOP.

≡ click ≡ "POOP" IS PROHIBITED LANGUAGE.

VERBAL WARNING.

The turds are processed in the--

"TURDS" IS INAPPROPRIATE FECAL SLANG.

SOAP WARNING!

ACK!

So your father went missing, and now you're trying to find him?

glub glub

OPTIMAL SECURITY MODE.

This SUCKS!

PROHIBITED LANGUAGE! THIRD AND FINAL WARNING!

TAPE!

mmmf

Violet?

Mmmkmeeuf?

WHAT THE FUDGE?!

PROHIBITED LANGUAGE!

WEZZZ

CLUB

GLUB

Elliot, I need your BUTTON-HUNTING skills to find that MUSKY part...

...then we can go search for my dad!

"WE"?

I'll HOT-WIRE the burger bus for MANUAL control!

That guy is a CRIMINAL!

No... He's my friend Zacchaeus!

Is he named after the wee, little man who climbed the sycamore tree?

Are you MOCKING me?!

TOSS

It's a biblical reference.

Well, I'm not religious. And I'm no "wee man."

I'm the LAST LIVING LUMPKIN!

Improbable. Lumpkins were famously TALL and LANKY.

Have you ever MET one?

They're also EXTINCT.

Not while I'm still kicking.

That's right.

I'm the ORPHAN OF MY SPECIES!

Hmmm... Hand-carved ivory swirlback.

Rare specimen.

MO-O-OM!

Maybe we should turn back.

Maybe you should grow a pair.

MOM? MOM MOM

DAD? DAD DAD D

Everything seems like I left it.

Your family LIVES here?!

It's F-F-FREEZING!

Get used to life in outer space.

I'm calling my mom!

Oh, yeah... duh.

BUSTED COM.

Are you saying we have NO CONTACT with the outside world?!

If the bus depot isn't there, then my mom can't get home from Shell-tarr...

Where am I?

Safe. With friends.

Friends?

For crying out loud, you are one feeble bird.

This space travel isn't good for you, is it, Elliot?

cough cough

I must admit...

We should return you to Shell-tarr before continuing on.

Yes, please.

Z

Wait...

I get it!

The Jirglebytes just wanted to retrieve the noggin of their comrade!

JIRGLEBITE

...

ZZZZ snork

ZZZ homina ZZZ

WUZZa ZZZork

Mommy, please don't be upset with me.

## 03

MAG/
GYRO
NAV

MAGNITUDES:

# TRIPLE THREAT

She's with Elliot.

≋WHEW≋ I thought she was LOST!

Why didn't they put her on the Ferry Wheel?

Oh, she and Elliot left the station to get fabric.

LEFT THE STATION?!

Safely accompanied by a top-of-the-line CHAPERDRONE.

SMILE SMILE SMILE AWAY THE RAINN

GNAW suckle

How did you let this HAPPEN?!

≋SNIFF≋

Did you SHOWER last night?

No, I was stuck on the Ferry Wheel-- WITHOUT MY DAUGHTER!

Thought so, because you're smelling a bit RIPE.

GEEYAH!

Elliot! Were you having a NIGHTMARE?!

AN ESCHATOLOGICAL VISION.

Scatological?

NO!

Well... kind of.

ESCHATOLOGY is the serious study of the END OF THE WORLD.

What's that AWFUL sound?

That's your ride back to Shell-tarr!

A tempest rose at sea, and only when the sailors tossed Jonah from the ship did the sea become calm.

Here goes...

Perhaps I'm this mission's JONAH...

KSSSH

...and after you UNLOAD THE BALLAST, it'll be smooth sailing for you from here on out.

Sounds about right to me.

On the other hand, maybe there's some COSMIC REASON for me being here.

Maybe if I walk away, I'm simply fleeing my destiny.

Neither of us understand a WORD you're saying.

What I'm saying...

...is that despite common sense...

...I want to join you two.

But I sent out a BURGER BUS and CHAPERDRONE yesterday.

WITH TWO CHILDREN!

That may have been one of our final departures.

THE SPILL has blockaded primary interstellar thorough-fares.

How long before transportation is up and running again?

SUCKERMOUTHS and sanitation workers are presently being dispatched.

In the meantime, that BURGER BUS is Shell-tarr property.

If not returned intact, penalties will be accrued to your citizen credit.

Oh, she's not a citizen.

She's just a DAY LABORER.

Then her work permit is now officially REVOKED!

Ma'am, without your permit, you're prohibited from station grounds.

Let me make one last COM CALL, please!

I could call Tinder . . .

No. I'm not THAT desperate.

I AM that desperate.

This is what I was trying to explain to you earlier, Elliot.

My dad harvests whale "timber" that is processed into these energy nuggets at the SAWMILL.

That's where we're headed to look for him.

Get outta here, kids! These nugget dispensers been RAIDED DRY!

RAIDED?

It's a DISASTER, buddy. Everyone's stocking up on supplies.

A full-on LOOTING SPREE!

With lots of competition!

More NUGGET STATIONS this way!

DO YOU KNOW WHERE GAR IS?

Can't say I see much of him anymore... Other than at work.

THAT'S WHAT I MEAN.., IS HE AT THE SAWMILL?

I wouldn't know, Mrs. Marlocke. They "LET ME GO."
≥urp≤

YOU MEAN, LIKE, FIRED?!

yeah... Wasn't Gar?

NO. HE TOOK ON SOME SPECIAL CONTRACT.

AND NOW HE'S GONE MISSING!

Son of a... So much for union solidarity.

Your hubby dug himself his own hole.

PLEASE, TINDER. VIOLET RAN AWAY. I THINK SHE'S LOOKING FOR HER DAD.

VIOLET'S MISSING, TOO?! Why didn't you say something sooner?!

I'll round up the ol' gang!

NUNCHUCKS.

NUNCHUCKA
NUNCHUCKA

Dental floss.

ZZZZZZ

WZZZZZZ

NUNCHUCKA

NUNCHUCKA

And how are we planning to get anywhere in a decent amount of time in the shack?

You know... The shack is as fast as its PREY.

INCOMING FREIGHTER

BOOP

Boys, we gotta get that barrel installed before the NUGGET runs out.

So who was that guy back on the ROIDS?

I dunno. Just some dumb-butt gangbanger.

I see a resemblance.

Whatever, Nerd-bird.

At least he's TALL ENOUGH to be an actual Lumpkin.

STUFF IT, turkey baster.

I heard the thug say, "You owe me this one, LITTLE BRO."

FOR CRYING OUT LOUD.

"BRO" is an abbreviation of the familial "brother"--denoting blood relation or at least spiritual kinship and solidarity.

OKAY, YOU GOT ME!

HE'S MY OLDER BROTHER, ZUCCHINUS!

Older brother?

Zucchinus was a real troublemaker.

Consumed all of my parents' attention.

Ran away from home and joined that CRISPY CROAKERS gang.

Because of that, I was a crappy student, and my parents enrolled me in SPECIAL NEEDS SCHOOL on the moon Gonaz.

Special needs school?

Is that the extent of your academic training?

That's where I was when my home planet of Lumpapalooza was DEVOURED.

Now Zucchinus thinks I owe him, because he's the reason I ended up on Gonaz, and avoided the whale attack.

But the real reason we survived is because we're both LOSERS.

That's not true, Zacchaeus.

Only partially.

133

I miss the other Lumpkins.

I miss my mommalump and poppalump.

In some stupid way, I even miss the days when Zukey and I were best buddies.

*sniff*

# OCCUPATIONAL HAZARD

47

Elliot needs to sleep off that seizure!

PLOP

SQUISH

I've always wanted my own feathery hug-buddy.

Who are these WEIRDOS?

This is my GODFATHER, Mr. Tinder!

EAT SLEEP FISH

Lieutenant Gerome the Gnome Allen. You can call me Gerry, GG, Little G...

Lieutenant? Were you in the WAR?

DAILY LIFE IS A WAR, LAD.

I'm Gwumpky.

What kind of name is that?

NITRO

It means "STUFFED CABBAGE."

Looks like all the stations are on the move, too -- farther away from us.

Should we head back to the SAWMILL and wait for the SUCKERMOUTHS to deal with this mess?

NO WAY!

SLEEP FISH

The Sawmill is to blame for my dad being missing.

They assigned him to a TOP SECRET, CONFIDENTIAL mission!

I know the mission well...

Wait... What do you mean?

An elite team of LUMBERJACKS --which would naturally include me--

And MY DAD!

And your dad...

were recruited ...

to kidnap a baby whale.

KIDNAP?!

This KID could use a NAP.

WHY?!

Heck if I know. That's the "confidential" part.

A fool's errand of AHABesque proportions ...

Elliot! You're AWAKE!

Perhaps MY father knows something.

What are you talking about?

Are you sure you're okay?

Those SPASTIC FITS of yours are really freaking us out!

Before he abandoned me to work on the interplanetary laboratory, my father was researching the digestion of the space whales.

Is this related to TEST-TUBE PROTEINS?

slide

No. It's related to ENERGY RENEWAL.

You really are the most adorable bundle of fluff.

Give him some space. Can't you see he's had a mental trauma?

So what happened on the MISSION, Mr. Tinder?

You tell me. I declined to participate, and then I LOST MY JOB.

Lost my pension, lost my health insurance, lost my truck...

Yeah, well, we lost our TRIKE!

We did?

Been living in the SHACK with these two SLACKERS ever since.

But the BOSS MAN said the mission was a SUCCESS.

If so, where's the baby whale?

We could consult the FISH-FINDER.

Every fisherman's favorite gadget. Identifies the species... shows you where they're BITIN'!

FISH FINDER

S-P-A-C-E W-H-A-L-E

There's the herd. They stay together like that in a POD.

Let's widen the net.

SPACE...WHALE

BINGO.

A single whale isolated from the rest.

Gotta be the baby.

AND MY DAD!

OR it could be a ROGUE. Those ones are always the most brutal.

Looks like we'll find out if we don't shift directions.

GG, 180°!

But my dad!

Girl, there's a reason I turned down that kidnapping mission...

Because it's SUICIDAL!

A lumberjack's duty is to keep a safe distance from those beasts, gleaning the bounty in their wake.

Get too close? Well, space whales eat ships, asteroids... They devour ENTIRE PLANETS, for crying out loud!

AAARGH!

Zach knows.

I know, because the whales ate my school and then my friends were separated from me.

But I didn't let the whales win.

I made TWO BETTER friends.

The BEST friends a girl ever had!

Awww...

Drive carefully, Gerome!

Directions would help, CAPTAIN POOPYPANTS!

Mr. Tinder, are you gonna let the whales take your FRIEND from you?

Mr. Gnome, don't you wanna relive your glory days as a WAR HERO?

Mr. Cabbage, are you going to stand idly by while the SYSTEM exploits working class gentlemen like yourself for the insatiable energy appetites of the ELITE?

Appetites?

Do you mean I can win SNACKS?

If snacks are all that you love, then that's what you'll receive.

# BAIT & SWITCH

That's where the HERD ended up.

Looks like they're snacking on trash like an ALL-YOU-CAN-EAT BUFFET!

Whale-made waste or man-made waste? We're doomed either direction...

There's another whale --a faint blip-- on the other side of the Mucky Way.

≡ Sniff ≡ THAT must be the baby whale then.

Why there? And HOW?

LAB STAR.

The interplanetary laboratory. It must be.

They're strategically hiding the baby behind a BARRIER of garbage.

Now'd be a good time to radio in those reinforcements.

We don't care about your precious "book" knowledge.

Obviously, it doesn't apply to real-world survival -- like getting out of this MESS!

If the whales were ANAL RETENTIVE like me, we wouldn't be in this predicament.

Furthermore, my dear special-needs-school-dropout, without an education, you'd only amount to an unkempt simpleton passing gas in a hand-cobbled hillbilly shack.

Why you...

...NERDY, PRANCY-PANTS, ASCOT-KNOTTED, RICH KID!

Oops.

Once again, brute force fixes the problem.

YAWN

Boys are so stupid.

SNAP

Elliot's right.

I would have grown up to be a useless deadbeat like these fools.

But you're the one that could have had a future.

You deserve what's left of this.

RUMMMMMBLL

Sounds like another craft passing by!

??? FLIP

BOOP

BRIT LAUNCH

PYOOR!

CLANK

Got some-thing!

I dreamt it.

A triangle-shaped CHARIOT.

Just before we were jostled awake.

THIS WAY!

What a CLAMOR upstairs!

Can you two open this?

You realize that's a SEPTIC TANK in there, right?

I have an inkling this Suckermouth has NOT been used for its designated purpose...

What about the fishin' buddies? Are we gonna abandon them?

You trust those MORONS to not get us snared in whale GOOP all over again?

Violet, your mother is worried to death about you.

We can get assistance at Shell-tarr.

But they aren't going to help us!

Our CHARIOT awaits at the end of this chute.

No. It's THIS chute!

You only pick the RIGHT SIDE because of your stupid superstitions!

My calculations are more sophisticated than yours.

My SUFFOCATIONS are more CALCULATED than yours!

STOP FIGHTING, YOU TWO!

... there's still one family we can save.

Whatchyoo talkin' about?

...

The WHALES!

The whales.

? ? ?

We rescue the baby whale...

...and return her to her momma.

Rescue.

A.

Whale.

From Lab Star?

So I was saying...

CHOOOP

BOING BOING

THEY ATE MY ENTIRE SPECIES!

You're right, Zee.

The whale herds devoured Lumpapalooza.

This place has been ransacked.

But this baby whale wasn't responsible.

It probably wasn't even born.

Scandalous vandalism.

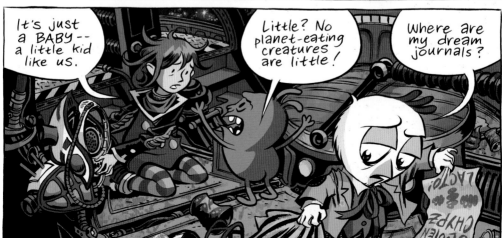

It's just a BABY-- a little kid like us.

Little? No planet-eating creatures are little!

Where are my dream journals?

You're proud of your Lumpkin heritage, right?

ORANGE IS THE NEW BLACK!

I swear I shelved them in this nook.

But when the other Lumpkins were alive, how did they treat you?

...

They called me the "RUNT of the litter."

Compared to the herd, the baby is the same.

Small, defenseless, exploited by its captors.

That baby whale ain't a BEACH BALL for some scientists to batter about!

The Crispy Croakers must have taken my journals!

Why, I'll personally dismantle that laboratory piece by piece!

THEY'VE STOLEN MY DREAMS!

The suction release valve is back up in the Suckermouth.

Then the only way to detach the trike is to go FULL MUSKY.

FULL MUSKY, FOR REAL?!

Everyone into the cockpit.

But I'm not ready to see my father...

You should be happy you still have a pappy.

My POP is DEAD. Get it?

Violet's dad, too!

Well...

maybe not...

but

probably.

Sorry.

I'm sorry, too.

You know... death is like OUTER SPACE.

What the--?

Too vast and dark to comprehend,

swallowing all lives into insignificance.

So, too, was my soul a BLACK HOLE of loneliness, until a couple of warm suns --TWIN STARS-- breached orbit and cast a swath of illumination upon the emptiness.

Sounds kinda like a poem, except it doesn't rhyme.

My father has long been estranged from me...

but you, Violet and Zacchaeus, feel FAMILIAL.

Just what are you trying to say?

I'm going free-range,

flying the COOP,

and following you two to the edges of the galaxy with all the dangers it has to offer!

AWW RIGHT! DROP YER DUMPLINS!

I'd rather be a RUNT than be LITTER!

Top off fuel from the main tank.

Seal cabin.

Disengage.

Wobbly!

# 06

## MAG./ GYRO NAV

MAGNITUDES:

# RED SHELL, BLUE BLOOD

## A·T·U·N·E

ACROSS THE
UNIVERSE NEWS
AND ENTERTAINMENT!

AFTER THREE DAYS AND THREE NIGHTS,
THE TORRENT OF TOXIC WHALE DIARRHEA,
TASTEFULLY BRANDED AS "THE SPILL,"
HAS BEEN LARGELY CONTAINED THANKS
TO FEDERATION SANITATION VESSELS.

THE SPILL

STATION-DWELLERS CAN REST
EASY KNOWING THAT COMMERCE
ROUTES HAVE REOPENED TO
REPLENISH THE NECESSITIES
YOU'VE COME TO DEPEND ON, LIKE:

(advertisement)

MEANWHILE, NONCITIZENS
AND DAY LABORERS ARE
BEING RELEASED FROM
ORBITAL RECESS TO
RETURN TO THEIR HOMES.

THOSE WITH NO HOMES
TO RETURN TO CAN BE
ASSURED THAT MANY
COMMERCIAL PRODUCTION
FACILITIES ARE BEING
CONVERTED, so to speak,
INTO DISASTER-RELIEF
REFUGEE CAMPS.

HMMM

These DETENTION BULBS are outgoing with the fleet of Ferry Wheels.

WAIT!

Where are you taking her?

Back to where she belongs.

This one belongs with ME.

243

What are you doing to her?!

We're taking samples of the digestive fluids.

Did you know that the enzymes within their ABOMASUM are potent enough to break down radioactive material?

This is INSANE! You need to sew her up before the whale herd gets here!

The herd?

The POD has made steady progress through the refuse barrier.

Alert the defense unit!

And restrain these distractions!

CLAMP CLAMP

CLAMP

You'd be better off an ORPHAN.

What are you, some sort of MONSTER?

No, but the whales are.

Ever since the petroleum, uranium, and STARDUST mines were depleted, we've depended on these beasts for their energy-rich excrement.

The whales' principle diet, of course, are planets-- many of them INHABITED.

DON'T REMIND ME!

The stations are safe, because they're mobile...

DON'T REMIND ME OF THAT EITHER!

URBANSUB
SHELL-TARR
ASTRORIA
HELIOSBORO

But the stations are only mobile as long as we have fuel.

Thus, the conundrum.

So you plan to artificially replicate the whales' digestive process, and spare the lives of those not privileged enough to live on stations.

Well, then perhaps it's a MATH LESSON.

"THREE TIMES" is the amount of power we have as a TEAM.

Of what use is such POWER?

WE CAN SAVE THE BABY!

I'll figure out the control console!

LOWER ME, ELLIOT!

258

## 07

MAG/
GYRO
NAV

MAGNITUDES:

RUDDER
00L

# FIN OR FLUKE?

She was just in a hurry to get to her MOMMA!

AWWWWW

YOU'RE ALIVE!

I feared I'd lost BOTH of you!

I'm sorry I ran away, Mom!

You don't need to apologize...

...but what you did scared the

WHALE CRAP!

out of me.

US!

It was also very BRAVE.

You kids did something no adult could manage...

YOU SAVED PAPA!

Now HE's the one that has some EXPLAINING to do!

I took on a special assignment -- a terrible mission -- but my debt to the federation oughtta be paid off.

We can finally score that station citizenship.

Stations are hollow shells...

You two are my HOME.

SNIFF

I still need to use the restroom.

So Adam and I took the first available Burger Bus out of Shell-tarr.

Along the way, we crossed paths with this loveable lot...

By then, we'd expended all the fight we had in us.

And we found we had more in common than differences.

We all love spaceships and video games and sports...

and PRINCESS LEIA!

And I LOVE this man!

He's what the fashion industry has been waiting for.

So elongated and androgynous and otherworldly.

THE LAST LIVING LUMPKIN!

heh heh shucks

Violet, we can't take care of every HANGER-ON in society.

I worked hard to get where I am so I don't have to CODDLE those who MILK the system.

PEOPLE GOTTA PICK THEMSELVES UP BY THEIR OWN BOOTSTRAPS!

But...

He's right, you know.

But Zacchaeus and Elliot --

RISKED THEIR LIVES for you!

Oh, I was talking about these dang FISHIN' BUDDIES of mine...

heh heh

HAW HAW

hee hee

Wait... what?

fin.

# epilOGue

# THANKS TO...

Violet, Azure, and Dan, for being the inspiration.

Lily Mason, Stella Sablan, and Joy Wurz, for their girl-hero expertise.

Adam Arnold, for his namesake, and Jeremy Tinder, for his likeness.

Jeffrey Alden, Lucie Bonvalet, Pegi Christensen, Chris Duffy, Alessandro Ferrari, Justin Harris, Georgia Hussey, Rebecca & Brian Hahn, David Naimon, and Ami & Jon Thompson, for being first readers.

Joshin Yamada, for the photos; Timothy Arp, for the spaceship model; Jon Thompson and Bolster, for the video.

Dave Stewart, for brilliant coloring and plenty of patience.

Phil Falco, Adam Rau, David Saylor, and the entire Scholastic team, for believing in the project.

PJ Mark, for being an amazing agent, along with Cecile Barendsma and Marya Spence.

My dear friends and family, for their constant encouragement.

You readers, who stick along for the ride.

And finally Sierra Hahn, for looking after my neurotic Elliot side and my impulsive Zacchaeus side. Also, for being the love of my life.

# CRAIG THOMPSON

is an award-winning graphic novelist best known for his books *Good-bye, Chunky Rice*; *Blankets*; *Carnet de Voyage*; and *Habibi*. He has received three Eisner Awards, four Harvey Awards, and two Ignatz Awards. Craig lives in Los Angeles, California.

# DAVE STEWART is an

eight-time Eisner Award–winning colorist best known for his work at Dark Horse Comics, DC Comics, and Marvel Comics.

Photo of the author by Joshin Yamada, with the real-life trike and the real-life Violet, daughter of Azure and Dan.